STELLA

QUEEN OF THE SNOW

MARIE-LOUISE GAY

(g)

GROUNDWOOD BOOKS
HOUSE OF ANANSI PRESS
TORONTO   BERKELEY

Groundwood Books / House of Anansi Press
110 Spadina Avenue, Suite 801
Toronto, Ontario, Canada M5V 2K4
or c/o Publishers Group West
1700 Fourth Street, Berkeley, CA 94710

We acknowledge for their financial support of our publishing program the Canada
Council for the Arts, the Government of Canada through the Canada Book Fund (CBF)
and the Ontario Arts Council.

Canada Council   Conseil des Arts
for the Arts   du Canada

ONTARIO ARTS COUNCIL
CONSEIL DES ARTS DE L'ONTARIO
an Ontario government agency
un organisme du gouvernement de l'Ontario

Library and Archives Canada Cataloguing in Publication
Gay, Marie-Louise
Stella, queen of the snow / Marie-Louise Gay.
ISBN 978-1-55498-071-0
I. Title.
PS8563.A868S7295 2010   jC813'.54   C2010-902462-1

Printed and bound in China

To David

Sam had never seen snow.
This was his first snowstorm.

"Isn't it beautiful, Sam?" asked Stella.
"It is very white," said Sam, "and it makes me sort of dizzy."
"Come on, Sam," said Stella. "Let's go outside."

"Is the snow cold?" asked Sam. "Is it hard and icy?"
"Snow is as cold as vanilla ice cream," answered Stella,
"and as soft as baby rabbit fur."

"Can you eat a snowflake?" asked Sam.
"Polar bears do," said Stella.
"They eat snowflakes for breakfast."

"With milk?" asked Sam.
"Yes," said Stella. "And sugar."

"Let's make a snowman, Sam," said Stella.
"Where does a snowman sleep?" asked Sam.
"In a soft, fluffy snowbank," answered Stella.

"What does a snowman eat?" asked Sam.
"Snowballs..." sang Stella, "snow peas...and snowsuits!"

"Do snowmen eat *green* snowsuits?" asked Sam.
"No," said Stella. "They only eat pink ones."

"Are you sure?" asked Sam.
"Let's go skating on the pond," said Stella.

"Where is the water?" asked Sam.
"The water is frozen," said Stella, "like a giant silver popsicle."

"Are the frogs frozen, too?" asked Sam.
"No," said Stella. "They are sleeping under the ice."

"Come on, Sam," said Stella. "Put on your skates."

"Not right now," said Sam. "I'm listening to the frogs snore."

"Hey!" said Sam. "Why is fog coming out of my mouth?"
"When it's this cold," said Stella, "your words freeze.
Every word has a different fog shape. See?"

"I can't read yet," said Sam.
"Then let's build a fort," said Stella.

"Where does snow come from?" asked Sam.
"Where does snow go in the summer?
How many snowflakes are there in a snowball?"

"I don't know, Sam," sighed Stella. "Come and help me."
"Just a minute," said Sam. "I'm counting the snowflakes..."

"Let's climb this mountain," said Stella.
"Why?" said Sam. "What for?"
"Then we'll slide down," said Stella.

"Will we go very fast?" asked Sam.
"Faster than a bird," sang Stella.
"Faster than an airplane."

"Will we be able to stop?" asked Sam.
"Stop?" said Stella. "Who wants to stop? Hop on!"

"I think I'll walk down," said Sam.

"Do dogs get cold?" asked Sam.
"No," said Stella. "Dogs wear fur coats."
"Do birds get goosebumps?" asked Sam.

"No," said Stella. "Birds wear snowboots."
"Like mine?" asked Sam.
"Yes," said Stella, "only much smaller."

"Let's make snow angels," said Stella,
"with wide feathery wings."

"Do snow angels fly?" asked Sam.
"Do snow angels sing?"

"Of course," said Stella. "Can't you hear them?"

"Yes!" whispered Sam.